GW01564170

PHILIPPE DRUILLET

THE 6 VOYAGES OF
LONE SLOANE

Jean-Marc & Randy Lofficier
translation

NANTIER·BEALL·MINOUSTCHINE
Publishing co.
new york

ALSO AVAILABLE IN THE SERIES:

$9.95

$9.95

$12.95

Add $2 P&H 1st item,
$1 each addt'l.
NBM
35-53 70th St.
Jackson Hts., NY 11372
**Ask for our complete catalog
of graphic novels.**

Lettering by David Jackson & Rachael Rodrigo
Printed in Hong Kong

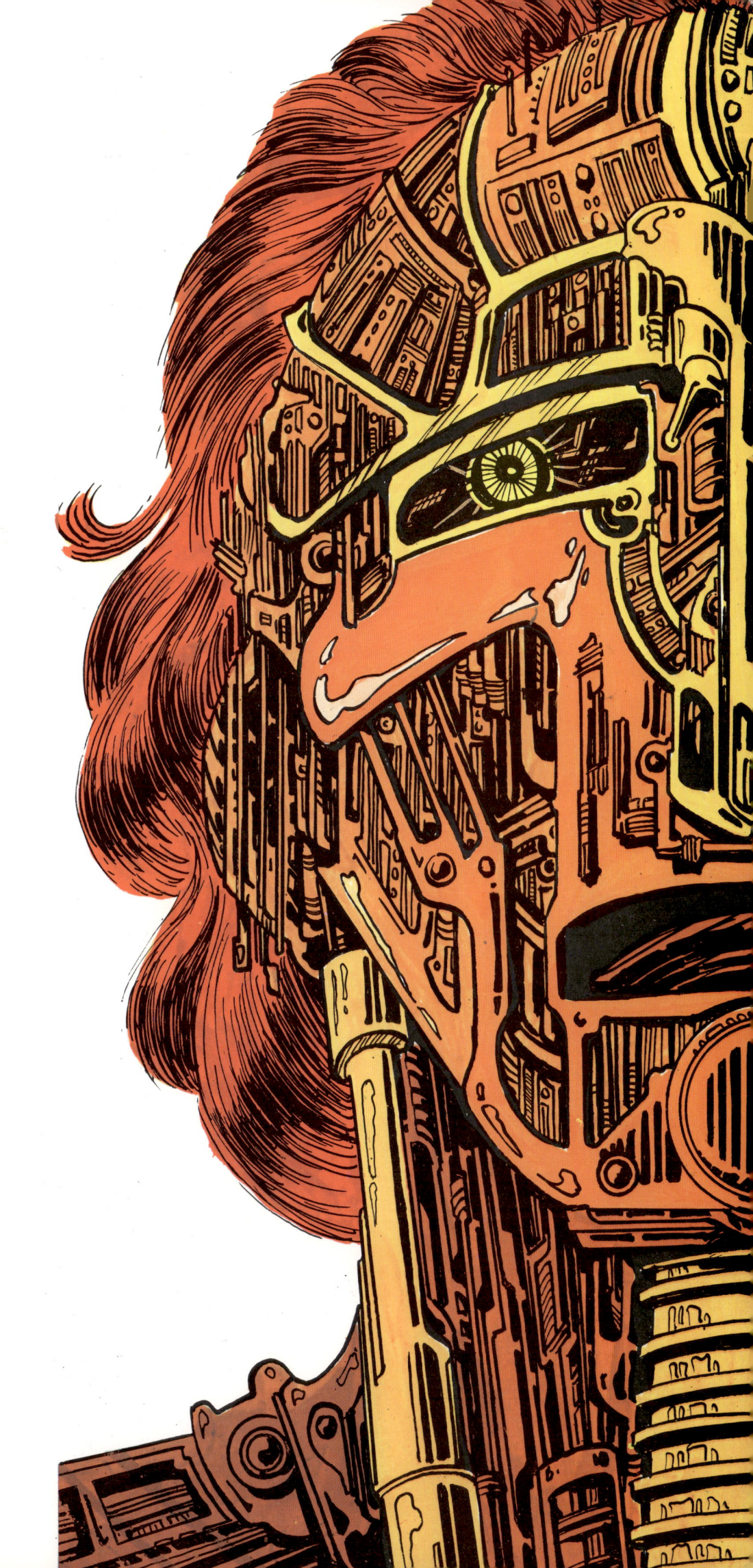

EXPLODE...

IN A BLINDING FLASH SLOANE'S SHIP DISINTEGRATES, BUT HIS BODY IS MIRACULOUSLY PRESERVED FROM THE RAVAGES OF AIRLESS SPACE BY A MAGIC MIGHTIER THAN SCIENCE. WHERE ONCE THE PROUD VESSEL STOOD, A MYSTERIOUS OBJECT APPEARS...

IT IS "OTAI", HE WHO SEEKS", A LIVING THRONE, CARVED OF STONE. THROUGH TIME AND SPACE IT HAS TRAVELED, ON A MISSION ORDAINED BY ITS MASTERS, THE DARK PRIESTS OF THE BLACK GOD, SEEKING A CREATURE TO BECOME THEIR "LIVING ONE". HERE, AT THE EDGE OF THE GALAXY, IT HAS FINALLY CAUGHT ITS PREY!

TIME AND SPACE LOSE ALL MEANING AS IOTAÏ TRANSPORT SLOANE. SLOWLY THE TAINT OF THE DARK GODS WHO ONCE MADE THE UNHOLY THRONE CORRUPTS THE EARTHMAN'S SOUL, AND HIS EYES BEGIN TO BURN WITH THE FIRES OF MADNESS.

"HE WHO SEEKS" FINALLY APPROACHES A WORLD, ANCIENT AND DARK AMONG THE STARS, DEVOID OF LIVING SOULS AND SEETHING WITH SO CONSUMMATE AN EVIL THAT EVEN SLOANE'S SPIRIT IS GRIPPED WITH TERROR...

WHEN THE EARTHMAN SEES THE TEMPLE-MOUNTAIN, DARK AND GARGANTUAN, BLOATING THE HORIZON, HE AT LAST UNDERSTANDS THE PURPOSE OF HIS ACCURSED JOURNEY.

3

...THEY WHO STOLE THE ELDRITCH SECRETS OF THE ANCIENT RACE WHO ONCE MADE THE THRONE...

I SEE ANGER IN YOUR EYES, "LIVING ONE".

DO NOT BE QUICK TO JUDGE US! WE TOOK YOU CAPTIVE, BUT WE HAD NO CHOICE!

OUR GODS ABANDONED US EONS AGO. WITHOUT THEM, WE ARE NOTHING, OUR RACE IS DOOMED!

BUT ONE OF OUR GODS STILL LIVES. WE HAVE THE POWER TO SUMMON HIM BACK, TO RESTORE THE GLORY THAT ONCE WAS OURS.

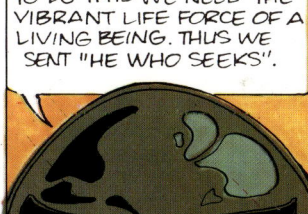

TO DO THIS WE NEED THE VIBRANT LIFE FORCE OF A LIVING BEING. THUS WE SENT "HE WHO SEEKS".

NOW YOUR LIFE WILL BE THE LIGHT THAT WILL GUIDE OUR GOD BACK FROM THE DARKNESS.

I DON'T CARE ABOUT YOUR GOD!

YOU'VE DESTROYED MY SHIP AND DRAGGED ME ACROSS THE UNIVERSE TO SAVE YOUR WORTHLESS LIVES! TO HELL WITH YOU!

TAKE HIM AWAY!

IRON-MASKED GUARDS DRAG SLOANE THROUGH THE TEMPLE-MOUNTAIN, ACROSS GARGANTUAN HALLS WHERE MUMMIES OF THE DEAD GODS STARE AT HIM, BEFORE FINALLY ABANDONING HIM IN A CELL. THE EARTHMAN'S MIND IS FILLED WITH A COLD FURY. HE HAS NOTICED THE OMINOUSLY EMPTY THRONE, WAITING FOR ITS DARK MASTER. HE KNOWS HE HAS NEVER BEFORE FACED SUCH DEADLY PERIL.

DURING WHAT MIGHT BE THE THIRD NIGHT, SLOANE IS AWAKENED BY INTENSE, SEARING LIGHT. IT IS AS IF THE UNIVERSE ITSELF HAS SUDDENLY INVADED HIS CELL.

THE GOD KINGS

LET YOUR EYES SEE, LET YOUR EARS HEAR, O "LIVING ONE"! THE CALL OF THE DARK PRIESTS HAS REACHED US! WE HAVE HEARD THE CRY OF DANGER ECHOING THROUGH OUR PALACES OF LIGHT! THE DARK PRIESTS HAVE LIED! THE GOD THEY WISH TO SUMMON WITH THE SPARK OF YOUR LIFE IS THE GOD OF DEATH AND DESTRUCTION ITSELF — THE "BLACK GOD"!

THEY HOPE TO BEND HIM TO THEIR WILL BUT THEY ARE MAD. THE "BLACK GOD" OBEYS NO ONE. HE WILL BRING CHAOS AND DOOM TO YOUR UNIVERSE. SUCH CANNOT BE TOLERATED. YET WE ARE FORBIDDEN TO INTERVENE. ONLY YOU, AN INSIGNIFICANT PAWN, CAN STOP THEM.

WE WILL GIVE YOU THE "ONE WORD" WHICH WILL CAST THE "BLACK GOD" BACK INTO THE ABYSS FROM WHICH IT CAME. WHEN YOU FEEL HIS EVIL ENTERING YOUR SOUL, YOU WILL SPEAK IT.

YOU WILL SPEAK IT ONCE, THEN FORGET IT! FAREWELL, O "LIVING ONE"!

IT IS TIME!

SLOANE IS THROWN INTO A TERRIFYING MACHINE WHOSE GARGANTUAN BELLY PULSATES WITH UNHOLY ENERGY, AND WHOSE MASS FILLS AN INCONCEIVABLY HUGE HALL. HIS BODY TWISTS AND ROLLS, SLAVE OF THEIR ACCURSED SCIENCE. HE BEGINS TO FEEL HIS LIFE FORCE EBBING AS IT IS USED TO SUMMON THE "BLACK GOD" FROM THE DEEPEST ABYSS OF THE COSMOS. SUDDENLY HE KNOWS THE CALL HAS BEEN HEARD. THE GOD IS COMING.

THE CEREMONY REACHES ITS APEX. SLOANE'S BODY IS SUBJECTED TO SPELLS OF INCREDIBLE MAGNITUDE. THE BARRIERS OF HIS MIND BEGIN TO CRUMBLE. THE EARTHMAN SENSES THE COMING OF THE "BLACK GOD" AND TRIES TO REMEMBER THE ONE WORD, THE GIFT OF THE GOD KINGS...

THE WORD! THE WORD! WORD! THE C...

BUT THE FATES HAVE NOT ABANDONED HIM. IN BLINDING FLASH OF LIGHT, SOMETH UNFORESEEN OCCURS. THE OVE FLOW OF MYSTIC ENERGIES IS ACCIDENTALLY GIV MATERIAL SHAPE. SLOANE FINDS BODY MULTIP INT INFINIT

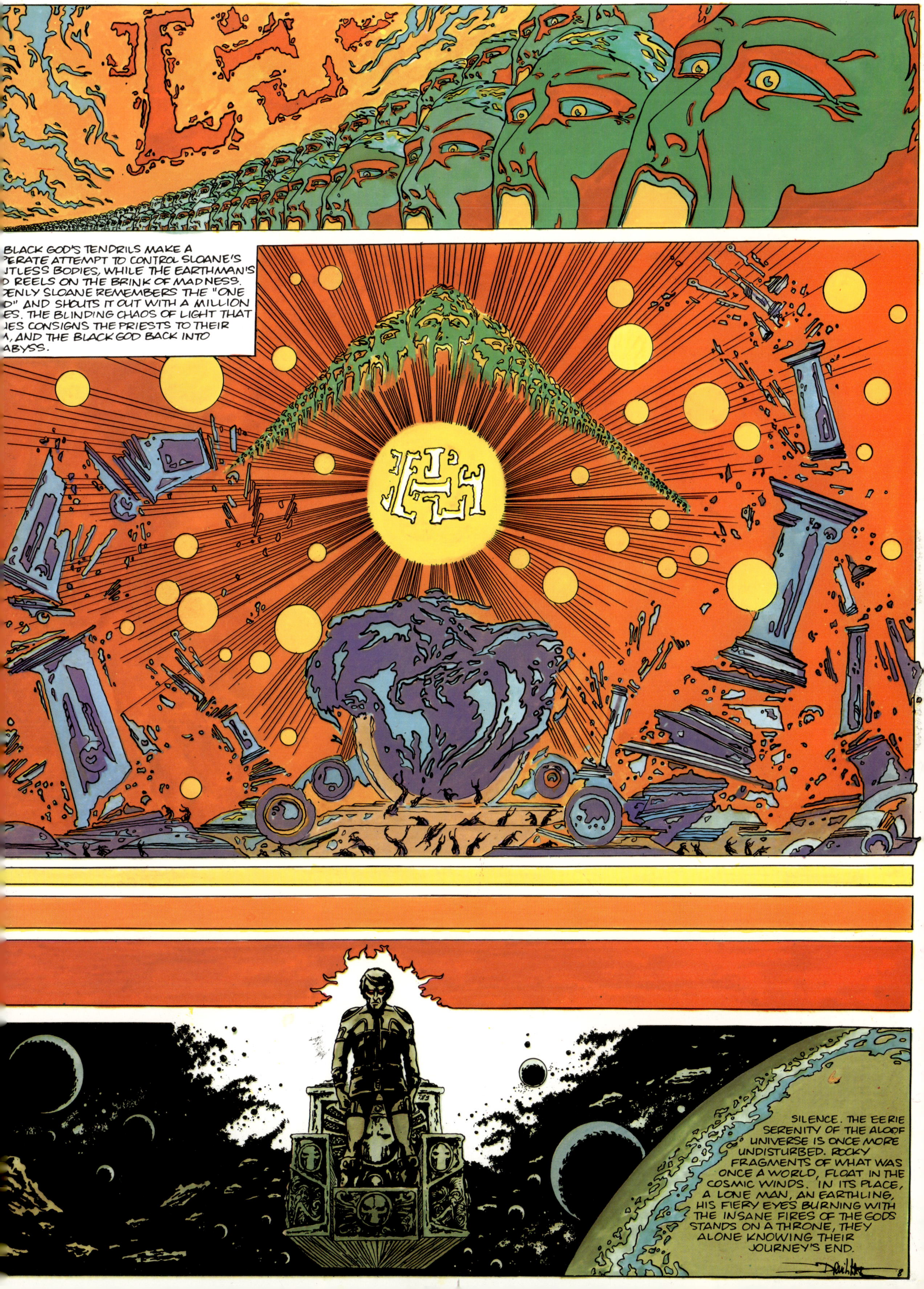

BLACK GOD'S TENDRILS MAKE A [DES]PERATE ATTEMPT TO CONTROL SLOANE'S [COUN]TLESS BODIES, WHILE THE EARTHMAN'S [MIN]D REELS ON THE BRINK OF MADNESS. [SUD]DENLY SLOANE REMEMBERS THE "ONE [WOR]D" AND SHOUTS IT OUT WITH A MILLION [VOIC]ES. THE BLINDING CHAOS OF LIGHT THAT [ENSU]ES CONSIGNS THE PRIESTS TO THEIR [DOO]M, AND THE BLACK GOD BACK INTO [THE A]BYSS.

SILENCE. THE EERIE SERENITY OF THE ALOOF UNIVERSE IS ONCE MORE UNDISTURBED. ROCKY FRAGMENTS OF WHAT WAS ONCE A WORLD, FLOAT IN THE COSMIC WINDS. IN ITS PLACE, A LONE MAN, AN EARTHLING, HIS FIERY EYES BURNING WITH THE INSANE FIRES OF THE GODS STANDS ON A THRONE, THEY ALONE KNOWING THEIR JOURNEY'S END.

THE ISLE OF THE DOOM WIND

ON A LONELY, FORSAKEN WORLD, THE MIGHTY SHIP OF SHONGA, PRINCE OF PIRATES, PLIES THE UNBRIDLED WATERS OF THE NINTH SEA, ALSO KNOWN AS THE SEA OF MADNESS...

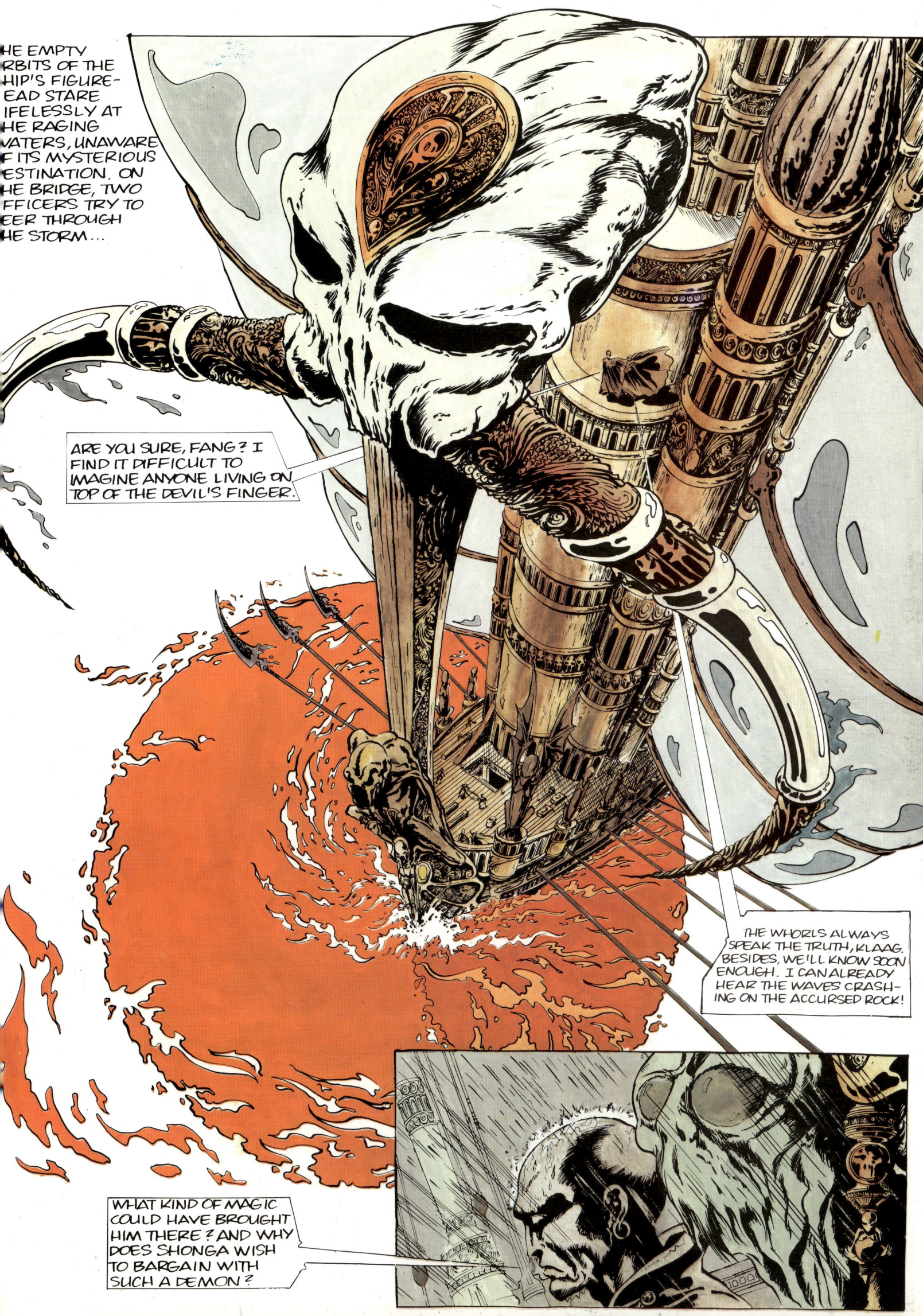

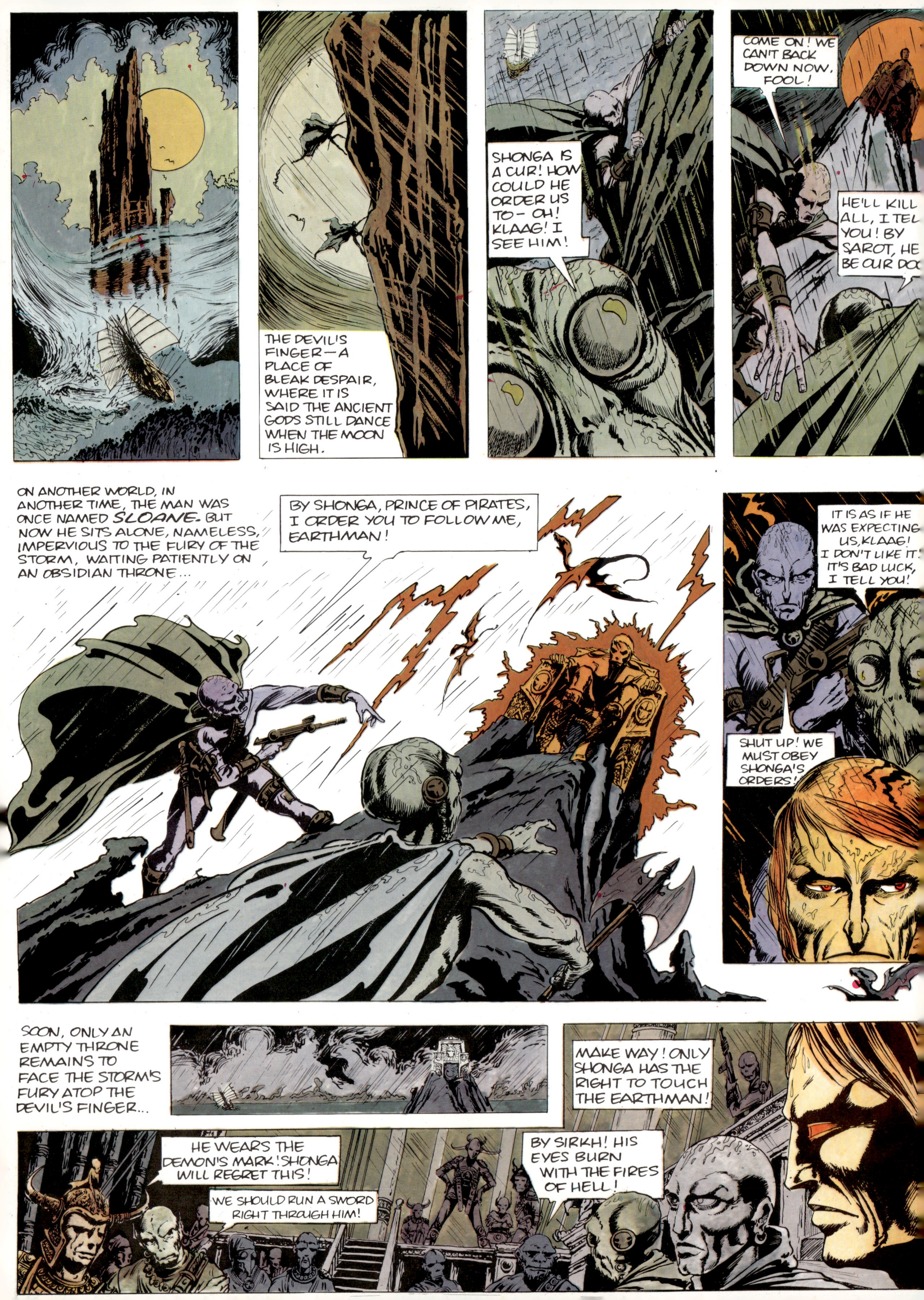

THE DEVIL'S FINGER—A PLACE OF BLEAK DESPAIR, WHERE IT IS SAID THE ANCIENT GODS STILL DANCE WHEN THE MOON IS HIGH.

SHONGA IS A CUR! HOW COULD HE ORDER US TO— OH! KLAAG! I SEE HIM!

COME ON! WE CAN'T BACK DOWN NOW, FOOL!

HE'LL KILL ALL, I TELL YOU! BY SAROT, HE BE OUR DO—

ON ANOTHER WORLD, IN ANOTHER TIME, THE MAN WAS ONCE NAMED *SLOANE.* BUT NOW HE SITS ALONE, NAMELESS, IMPERVIOUS TO THE FURY OF THE STORM, WAITING PATIENTLY ON AN OBSIDIAN THRONE...

BY SHONGA, PRINCE OF PIRATES, I ORDER YOU TO FOLLOW ME, EARTHMAN!

IT IS AS IF HE WAS EXPECTING US, KLAAG! I DON'T LIKE IT! IT'S BAD LUCK, I TELL YOU!

SHUT UP! WE MUST OBEY SHONGA'S ORDERS!

SOON, ONLY AN EMPTY THRONE REMAINS TO FACE THE STORM'S FURY ATOP THE DEVIL'S FINGER...

MAKE WAY! ONLY SHONGA HAS THE RIGHT TO TOUCH THE EARTHMAN!

BY SIRKH! HIS EYES BURN WITH THE FIRES OF HELL!

HE WEARS THE DEMON'S MARK! SHONGA WILL REGRET THIS!

WE SHOULD RUN A SWORD RIGHT THROUGH HIM!

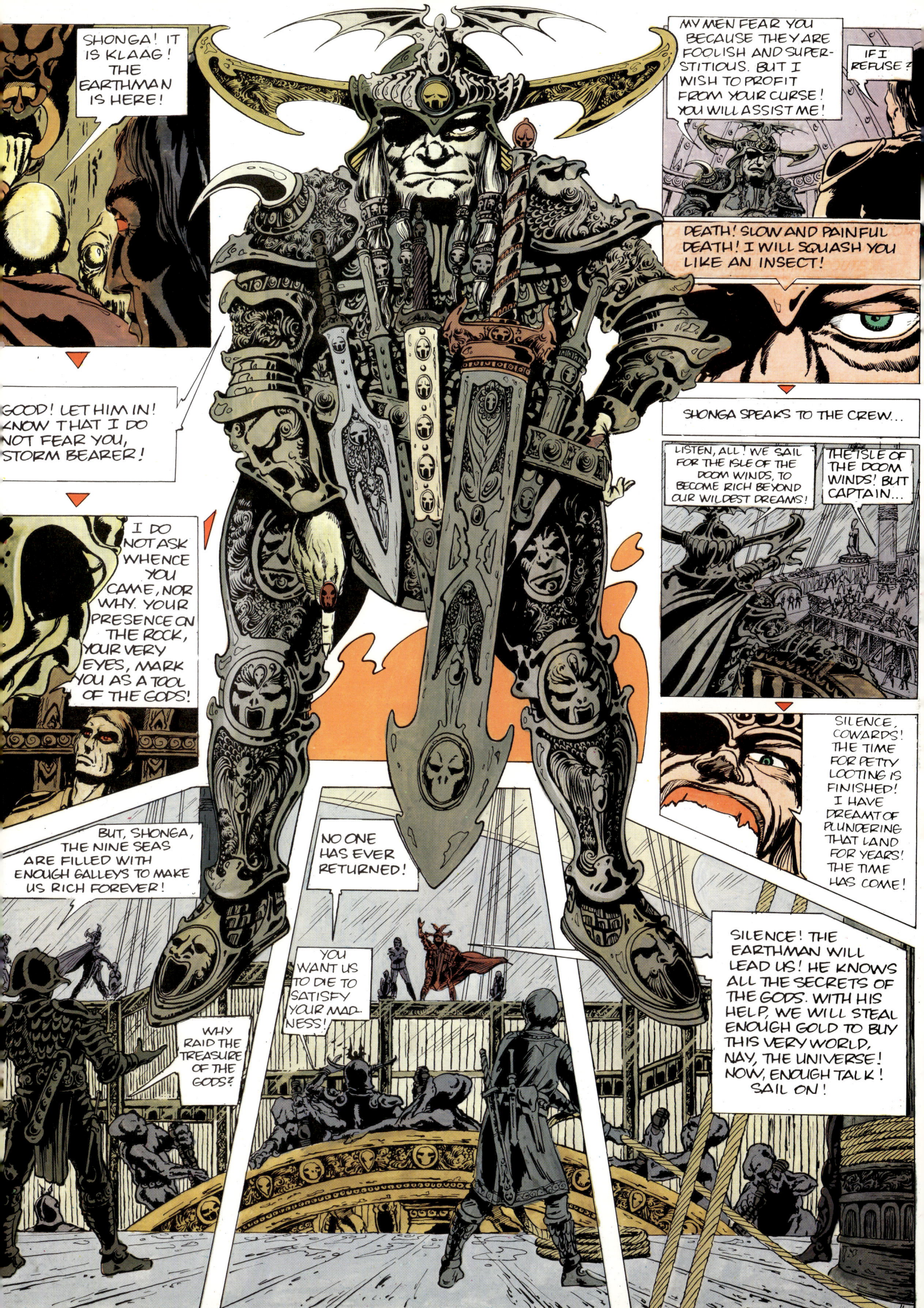

LED BY THE ONE WHO KNOWS, THE SAVAGE HORDE CROSSES THE VAST OCEAN...

...GREED CAUSES THE PIRATES TO FORGET THEIR FEARS. WITH THE EARTHMAN'S GUIDANCE, THEY AVOID NIGH-INVISIBLE REEFS AND LAND SAFELY AT A CREEK LINED WITH DEAD GODS' STATUES. HE WHOSE NAME WAS ONCE SLOANE, AND WHOM SHONGA THINKS HE HAS MASTERED, KNOWS THAT NONE WILL RETURN...

HERE BEGIN THE GREAT COSMIC CURRENTS. YOUR BODIES, YOUR SOULS, YOUR VERY LIFE FORCE WILL BECOME THE SEEDS THAT WILL BECOME GOLD, AND LIFE, AND LIGHT, AND MATTER, DISPERSED THROUGHOUT THE INFINITY OF SPACE...

ONE DAY, A MILLION YEARS FROM NOW, YOUR WANDERING ATOMS WILL GIVE BIRTH TO A NEW BREED OF MEN, AND MAYBE SOME OF THEM WILL COME HERE AND AGAIN BEGIN THE GREAT LIFE CYCLE. GOODBYE! I TRADED YOUR SOUL AND THOSE OF YOUR MEN TO THE GODS SO THAT I MAY RETURN TO MY OWN KIND, FREE OF THEIR DEVASTATING CURSE.

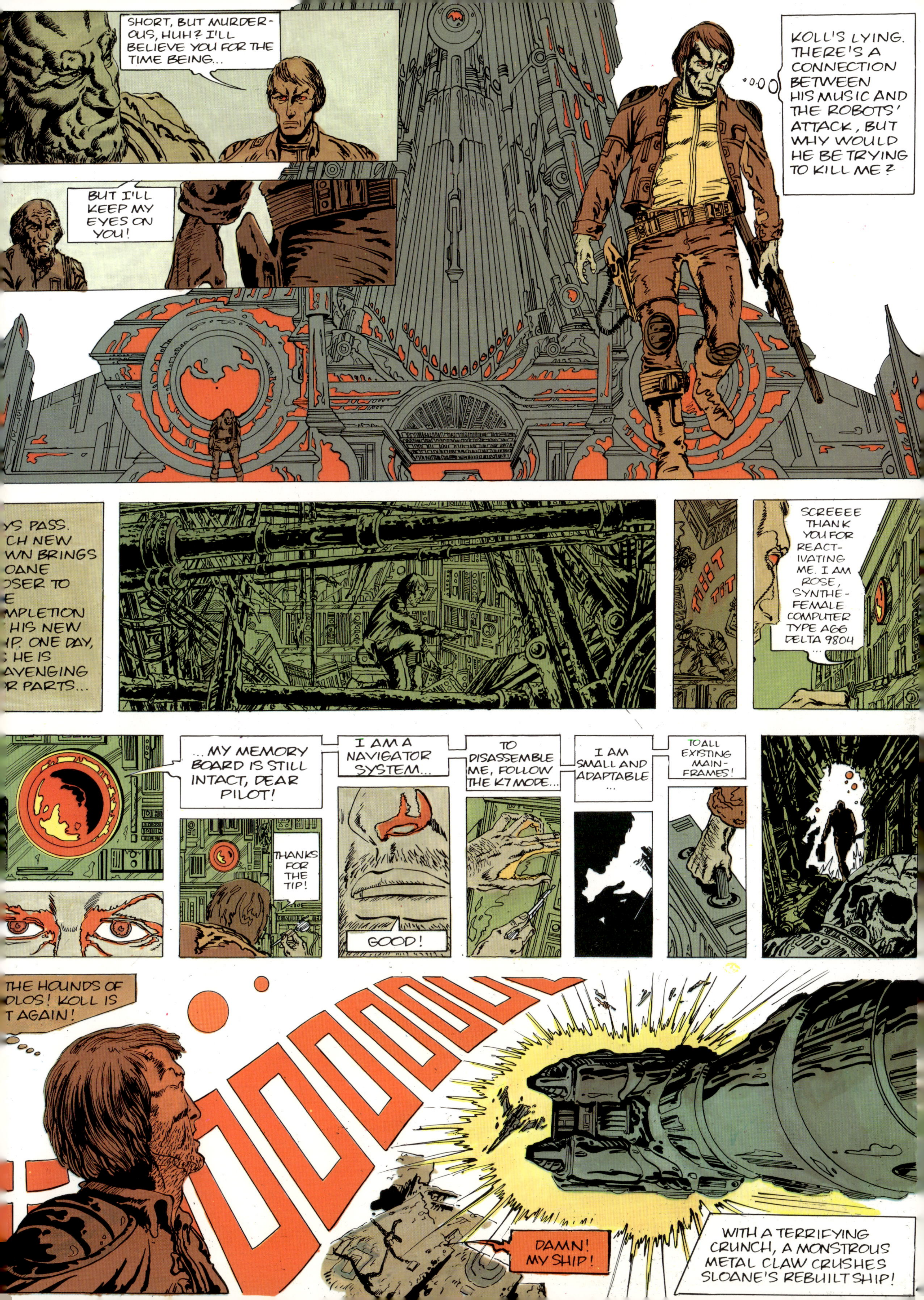

SHORT, BUT MURDER-OUS, HUH? I'LL BELIEVE YOU FOR THE TIME BEING...

BUT I'LL KEEP MY EYES ON YOU!

KOLL'S LYING. THERE'S A CONNECTION BETWEEN HIS MUSIC AND THE ROBOTS' ATTACK, BUT WHY WOULD HE BE TRYING TO KILL ME?

YS PASS. CH NEW WN BRINGS OANE OSER TO E MPLETION HIS NEW IP. ONE DAY, S HE IS AVENGING R PARTS...

SCREEEE THANK YOU FOR REACTIVATING ME. I AM ROSE, SYNTHEFEMALE COMPUTER TYPE A66 DELTA 9804...

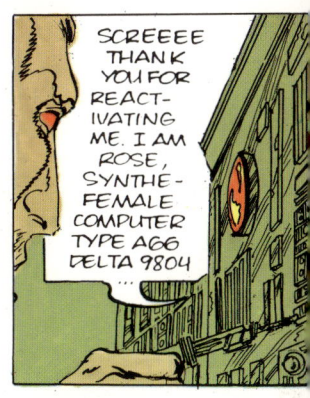

...MY MEMORY BOARD IS STILL INTACT, DEAR PILOT!

I AM A NAVIGATOR SYSTEM...

TO DISASSEMBLE ME, FOLLOW THE K7 MODE...

I AM SMALL AND ADAPTABLE...

TO ALL EXISTING MAINFRAMES!

THANKS FOR THE TIP!

GOOD!

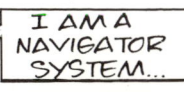

THE HOUNDS OF DLOS! KOLL IS T AGAIN!

DAMN! MY SHIP!

WITH A TERRIFYING CRUNCH, A MONSTROUS METAL CLAW CRUSHES SLOANE'S REBUILT SHIP!

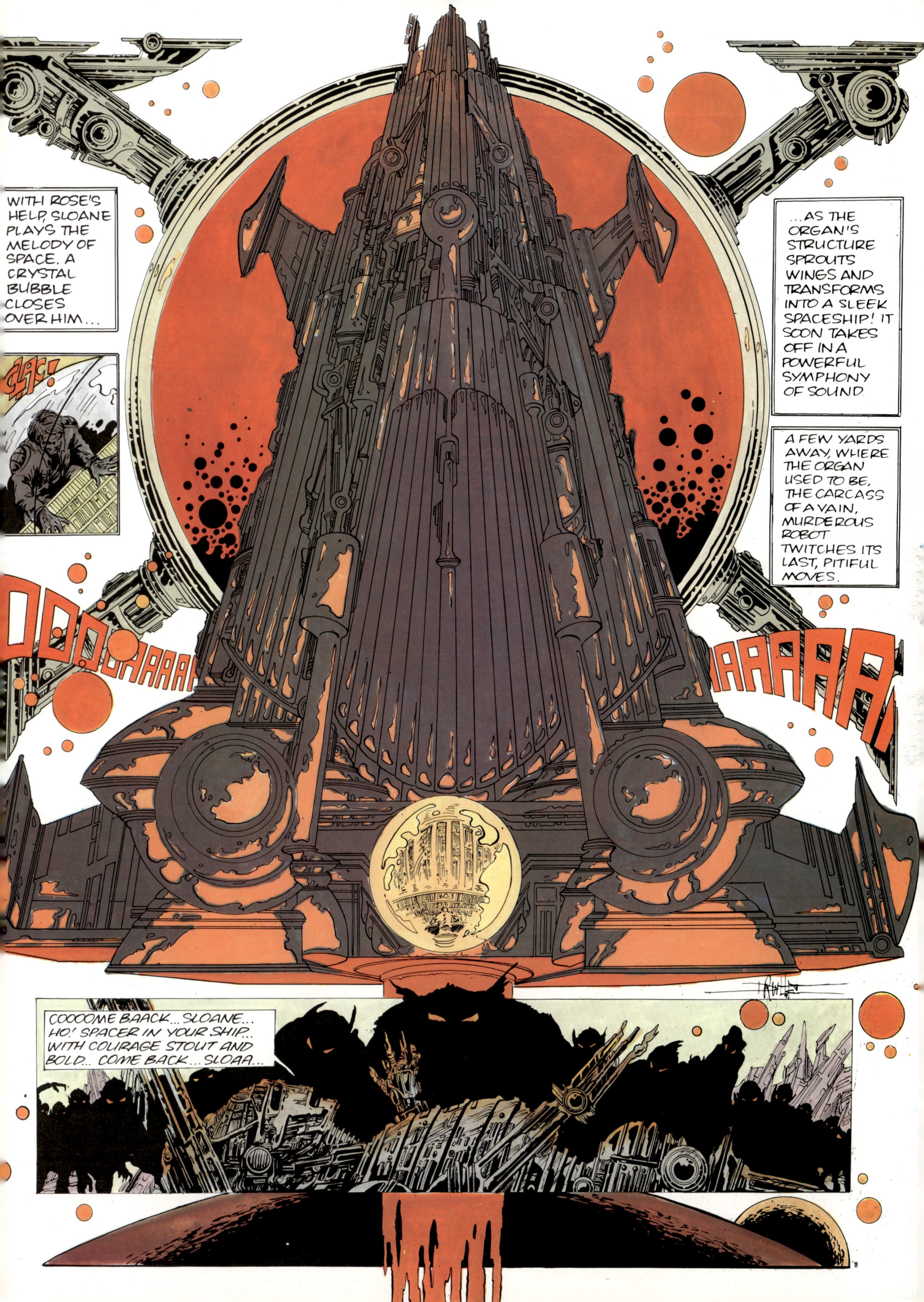

WITH ROSE'S HELP, SLOANE PLAYS THE MELODY OF SPACE. A CRYSTAL BUBBLE CLOSES OVER HIM...

...AS THE ORGAN'S STRUCTURE SPROUTS WINGS AND TRANSFORMS INTO A SLEEK SPACESHIP! IT SOON TAKES OFF IN A POWERFUL SYMPHONY OF SOUND.

A FEW YARDS AWAY, WHERE THE ORGAN USED TO BE, THE CARCASS OF A VAIN, MURDEROUS ROBOT TWITCHES ITS LAST, PITIFUL MOVES.

COOOOME BAACK... SLOANE... HO! SPACER IN YOUR SHIP... WITH COURAGE STOUT AND BOLD... COME BACK... SLOAA...

A VARENKOR

IN THOSE DAYS, THE GARGANTUAN WALLS OF THE STARBRIDGE WERE THE DOMAIN OF TORQUEDARA VARENKOR, SORCERER SULTAN OF SPACE, WHO DOMINATED THE SPACE LANES LEADING TO THE HUMAN IMPERILIM. TORQUEDARA WAS BORED, AND SO AMUSED HIMSELF BY TRAPPING UNWARY TRAVELERS, PLAYING FOR THEIR SOULS IN A COSMIC GAME OF HIS OWN DESIGN…

ROSE IS LOST, BUT TORQUEDARA WILL PAY FOR HER SACRIFICE DEARLY — AS I PROMISED HIM HE WOULD!

THE DARK HALF OF YOUR SOUL WILL TRICK THE CHAMPION...

...INTO BELIEVIN HE HAS CAPTURED YOUR TRUE SELF

I'VE GOT TO STEAL A DRAGON AND ESCAPE! THIS GUARD HAS HIS BACK TURNED...

MEANWHILE, TORQUEDARA'S CHAMPION HAS BROUGHT ITS PRIZE BACK TO ITS MASTER, NOT REALIZING THAT IT WAS NOT THE SOUL OF THE EARTHLING!

ZZZZ!! ZZZ!!

AS SLOANE FLIES AWAY, HIS DARKSOUL, A DEADLY BOMB PRIMED BY ROSE, EXPODES IN THE FACE OF THE SORCERER SULTAN, OPENING A HUGE BREACH IN THE STARBRIDGE. TORQUEDARA VARENKOR, DARK PRIEST OF THE GODS, WILL NEVER AGAIN EXACT HIS PRICE FROM INNOCENT TRAVELERS.

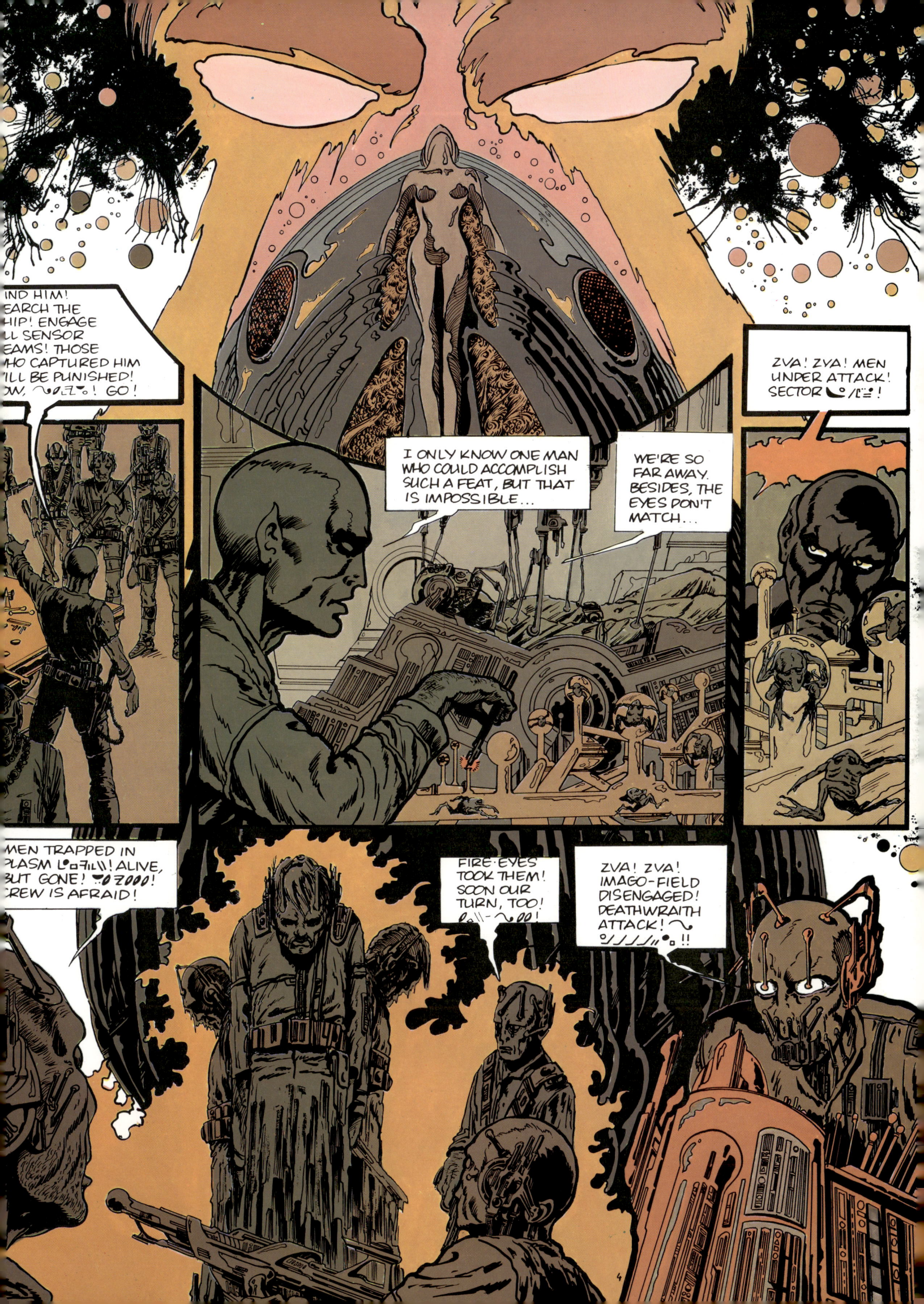

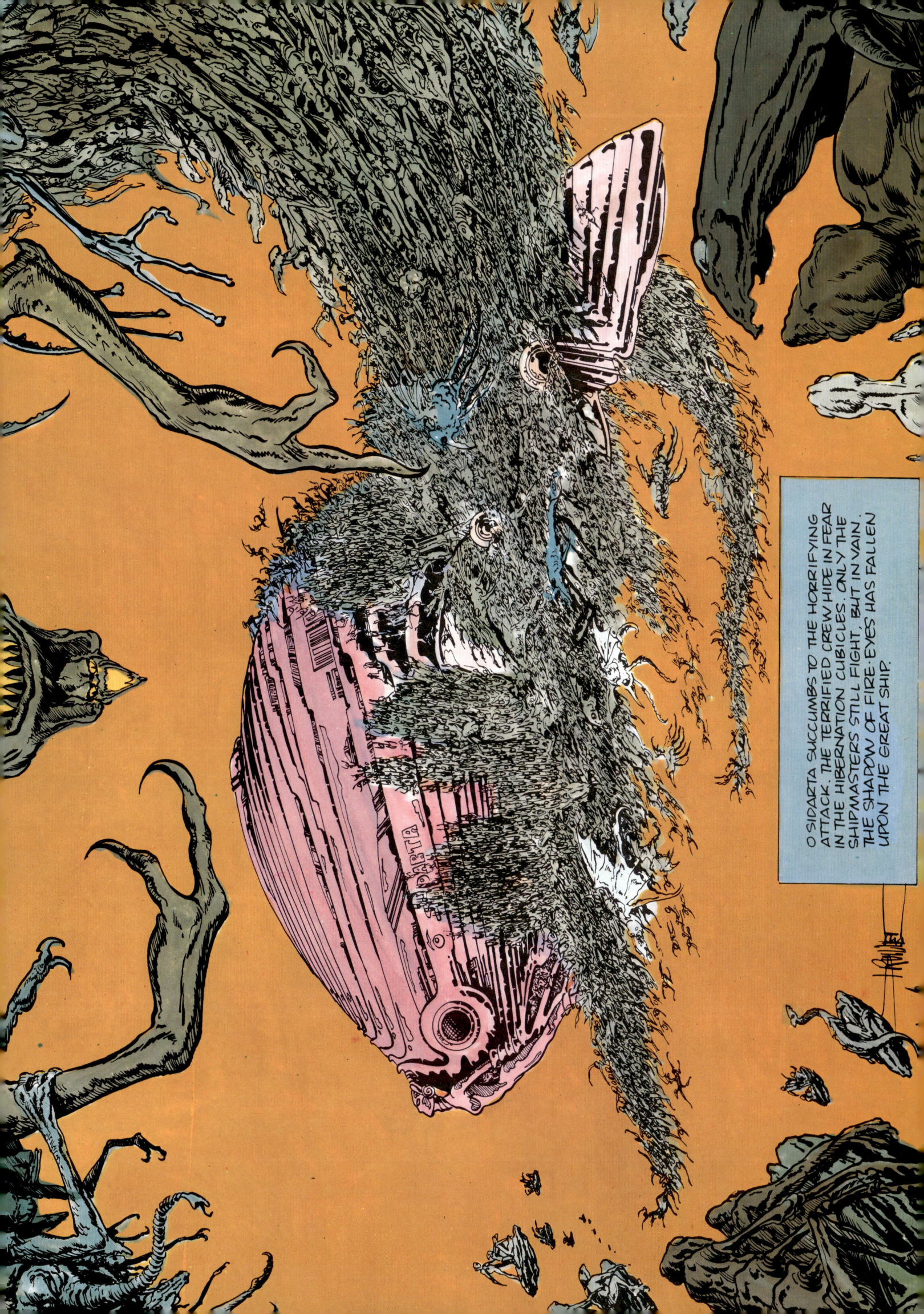

O SIDARTA SUCCUMBS TO THE HORRIFYING ATTACK. THE TERRIFIED CREW HIDE IN FEAR IN THE HIBERNATION CUBICLES. ONLY THE SHIPMASTERS STILL FIGHT, BUT IN VAIN. THE SHADOW OF FIRE-EYES HAS FALLEN UPON THE GREAT SHIP.

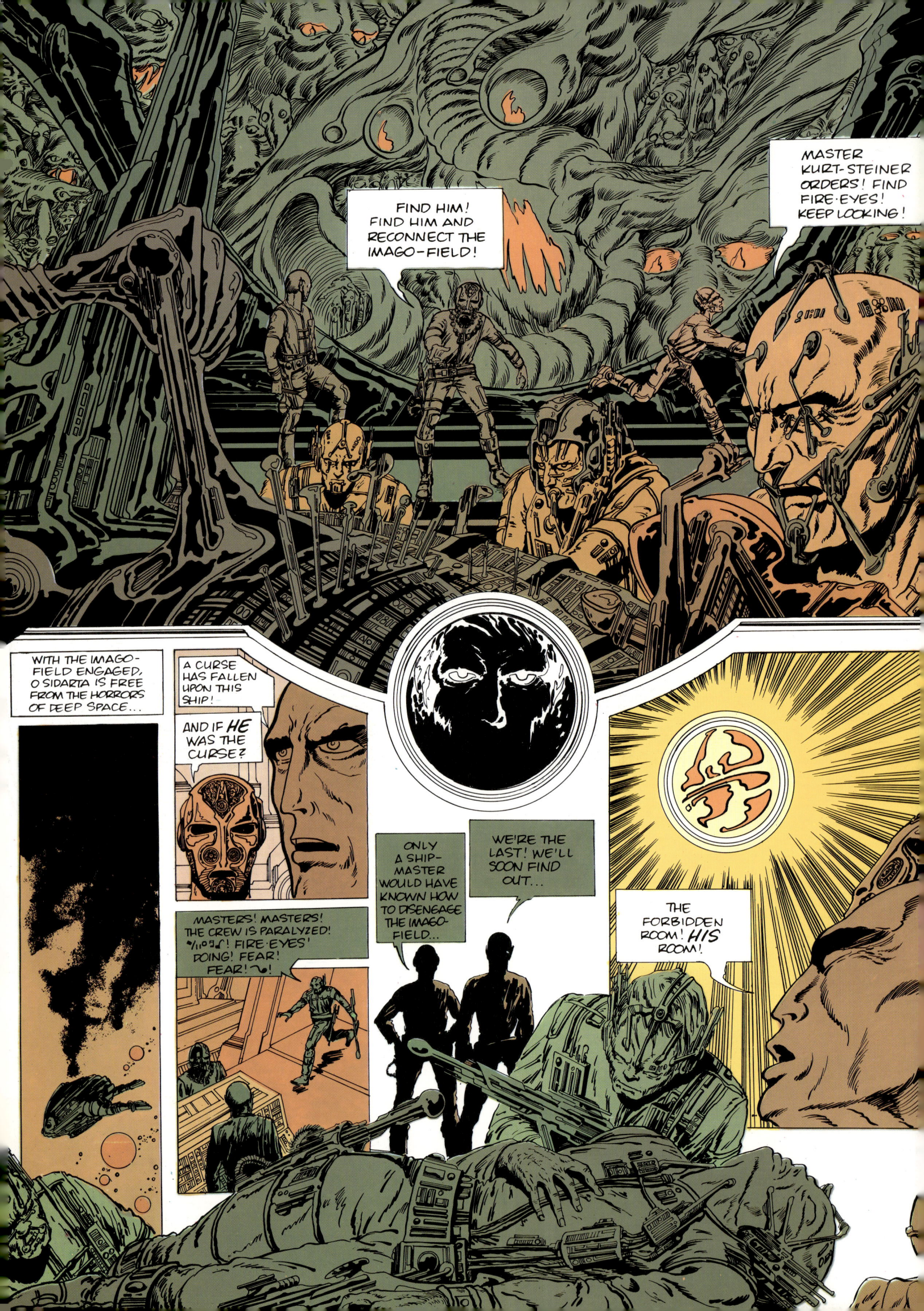

RA

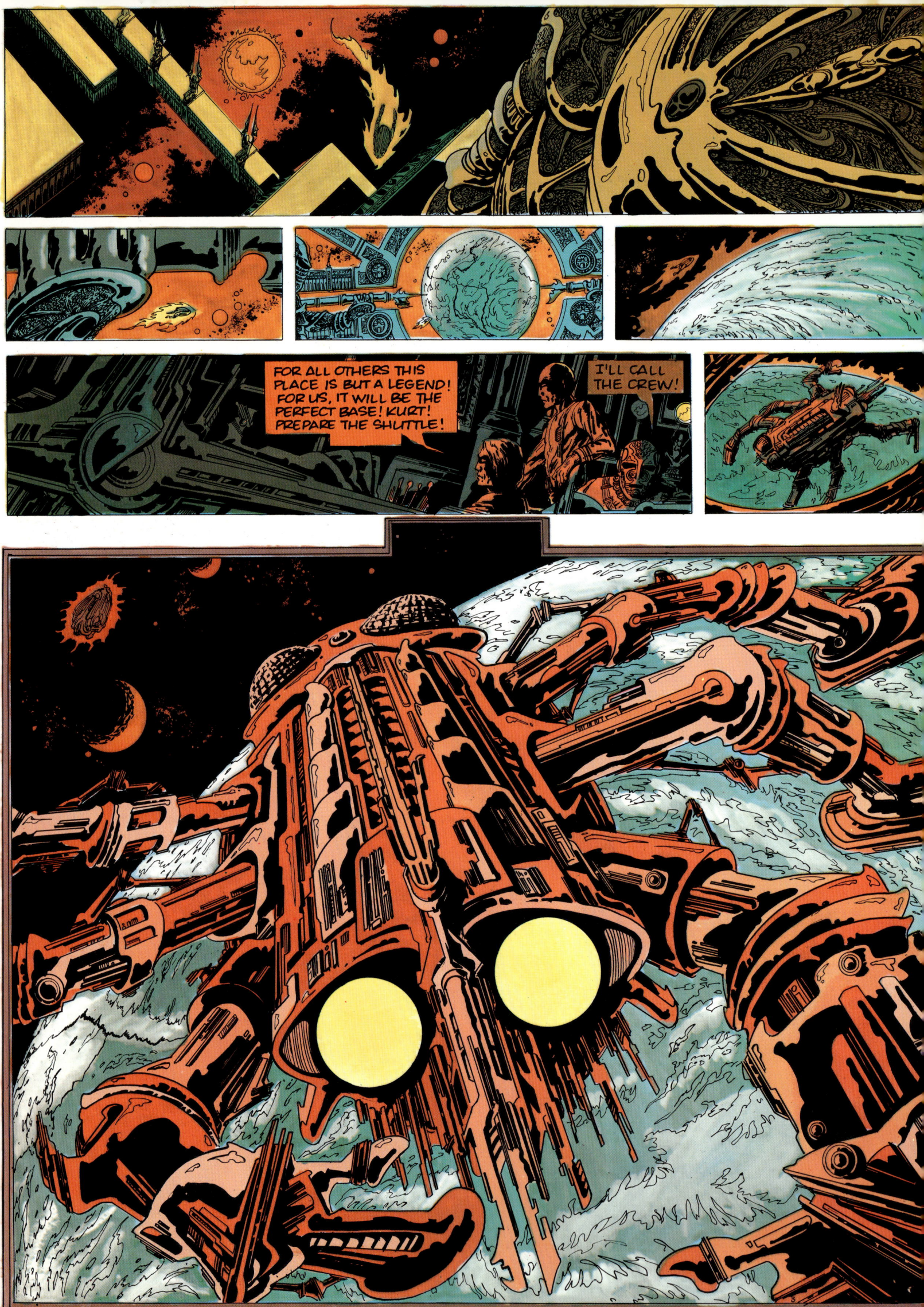

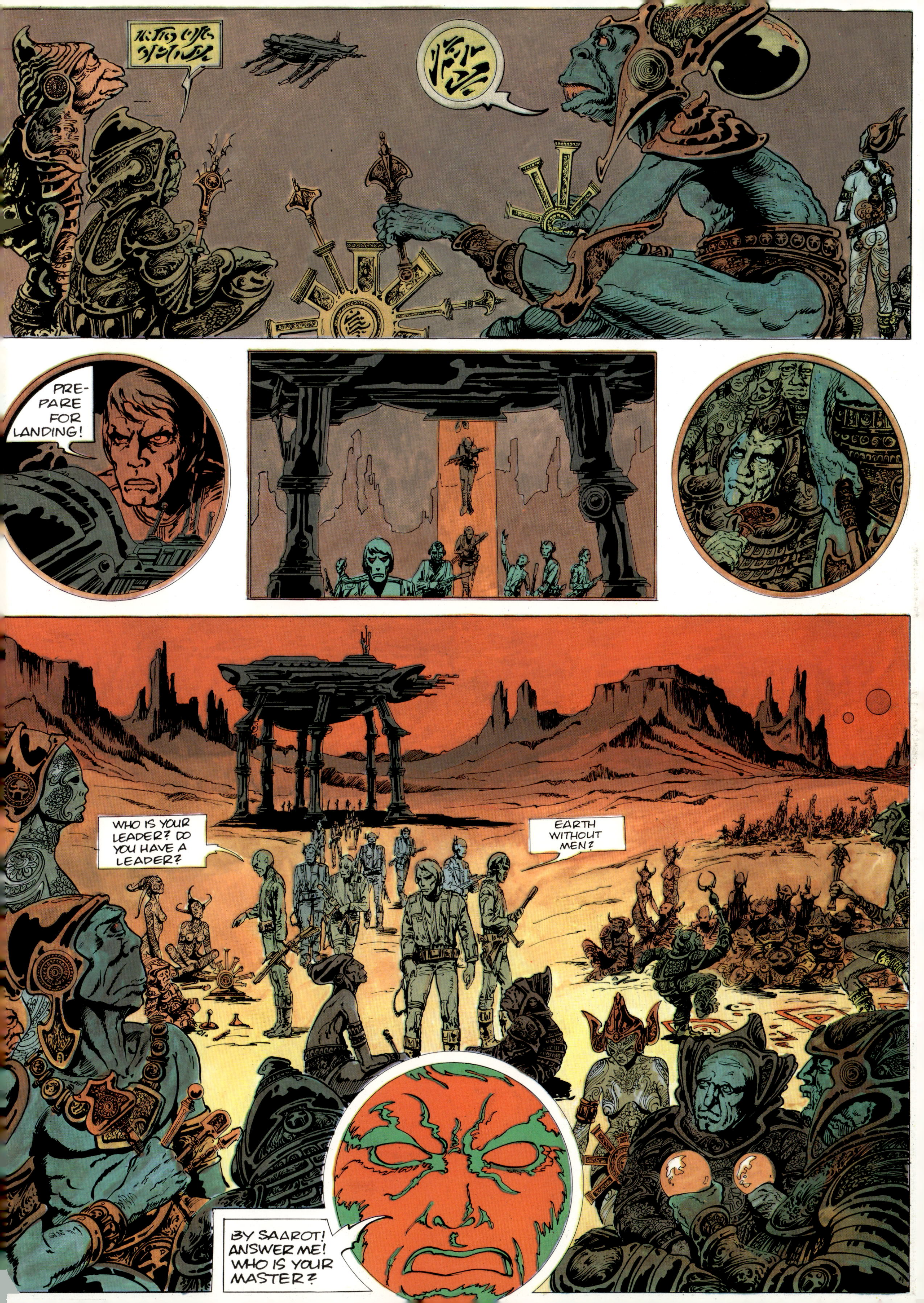